# ORANGE AND PEACH

A Book About Love

# INTRODUCTION

Orange and Peach is a collection of poems that I have written over the years for Delilah. Delilah is a person who means the world to me (as you would learn from reading the poems) yet she doesn't exist outside of this book.

Delilah is someone who I have met at every stage of my life. I met her when I was a child, during my early school years, in college and even after that.

And every time I meet her, I fall for her. She is what I would define as the projection of love for me. She doesn't exist, yet she does.

I have written these poems over the course of several years as a hobby, keeping Delilah in my mind. She is my imperfect perfection, my own creation. My writing style has changed over the years so you would be treated with different kinds of patterns, styles and themes.

Read with love.


Sheibban Sheikh Pervez

# CONTENTS

# THE CURSE

For a while now, I know about my curse.

It is a curse that had always existed.

It is a curse that I always knew about.

My curse is my own nature.

A nature that is forgiving and gentle.

Even to the most distant people,

My curse makes me value each interaction.

I forgive, I forget, I share happiness at my own cost.

But I realise.

Not everyone should see that side.

If they haven't earned it yct.

I know this and I want to follow this.

However, I can't control it.

I can't be selective of my forgiving nature.

And that is my curse.

# LE MORDE

This life, we come and go.

Little do we know, what it has to show.

Life is about friendship and love.

To transform you into a lovely dove.

People they come, people they go.

Just like the yearly winter snow.

Learn what we must from people that hurt.

Hate is an emotion that isn't worth the pert.

I speak from experience and logic and belief.

A person who hurts you is hurt himself indeed.

A friend in need is a friend indeed.

Rare are the occasions when this is the deed.

How would you like a life full of love?

A life without hatred, Jealousy or Distrust.

The beauty lies in your heart itself.

It's all about you and yourself.

Forgive your enemy and let him live another day.

Betrayed and guilty, that's how he will pay.

Enemy of enemy is a friend maybe.
But has hatred ever produced a good thing to be?

I am but a human, with a voice in my heart.
Using this voice is a work of art.
We look up to see the stars shine.
But forget that so do people, high on wine.

What is life, if not a journey.
What's the destination? You may ask maybe.
I don't have answers, only questions indeed.
Discover yourself is the answer you may seek.

A life without friends is like a river without fish.
Why move on when there is nothing that exists.
Emotions may weaken a man but remember.
Weakness is just the spark to the ember.

Who am I to come here and preach?
You are my student, I'm just here to teach.
Life isn't about sucking up and getting hurled.
It's about moving on and exploring the world.

# WITH ME

When I'm with you, the world seems brighter.

It feels happy, fun and beautiful, you make it all lighter.

Your smile wakes me up, your words my morning bell.

Your touch is electric, it's almost like I'm in a spell.

I feel different this time, I feel complete.

When I'm with you, the horizon and sea seem to meet.

You add colour to my dark world, like a beautiful crayon.

I just want to hold you forever in our own little haven.

You are so beautiful, inside and out.

I feel my darkest fears rest, when I see you, there's no doubt.

I'm so glad I found something genuine, in a world full of craftiness.

You, my love, are my little moment of happiness.

# THE YOUNG MASTER

Everyone deserves a friend, everyone needs one.

I think you two were one of my first under this lonely sun.

As the years passed, we distanced and grew.

Only once school ended did I realise you.

You shifted away but we became better friends.

I hope we can start again and make amends.

I do not know about you, but I feel so.

You were and are a close friend, just so you know.

This is a little birthday present, from me to you.

Let us toast again to someone born so true.

You were always so cheerful, so full of laughter.

Hope you stay the same, our young master.

# ONE AND ONLY

Everyone has a crush; everyone deserves to love.

Some stay forever, some just a quick buck.

But the moment does not matter nor does the time.

You are the only thing that does, and you are mine.


You, your name means friendship and love.

You are my everything, you are my little dove.

I cannot love or care about you anymore than this.

Because even if the sky was the limit, I have already crossed it
over into the abyss.


Each day we talk, a little more, a little less.

One text from you makes my heart go bless.

I cannot explain these feelings, nor will I be able to.

All I know is that I just want to say, " I do".

# MORNING DOVE

We grew up together, same class, same friends.

Our friendship became stronger, irrespective of ourselves.

I started to fall for you, thinking you are the one.

I knew that if I had you, the world was won.

We started talking more, a little here, a little there.

Each time was a different spark, each day a different flare.

Ultimately one day, I mustered up my courage and confessed.

You just heard me and declined, thinking it's for the best.

Time flew, we started talking again.

This time, I planned to stay on and make you, my gem.

I never realised if this was friendship or love.

But you will always be, my mourning dove.

# THE STORY IN MY EYES

The story in my eyes.

Each day, I muse my way.

I drag along, pleasing they.

I wish for an escape, a route.

I wish that I had my shoot.


When I finally close my eyes, I see it.

I see a story, a dream, I admit.

The story is about me and her, the one.

Her name is none but with her, I have won.


She shows me a story, a story in my eyes.

A dream of a life, where the sun only rises.

I chase that dream; I chase it with all my might.

But the more I chase, the more the fight.


She could do it; she can change my life.

She can show me a dream, in my eyes.

She is my goal, my destiny, my end.

And just to extend, she's my best friend.

Her story, her dream is what frees me.
It frees me from this shell, it's the key.
How can she be so beautiful, so kind?
Her heart is gold, she's, my bind.

The story in my eyes, she's the light.
Conversations with her are endless, such are the nights.
I wish I can continue it forever; I wish for it to be.
But she's my best friend, that she will always be.

So, here's to a story of friendship, not love.
A story about a selfless deep bond of us.
The bond shall remain, it's our identity.
But how beautiful would it be if it becomes our destiny.

# DELILAH

Like a sailor aboard a new journey.

I entered the voyage, having some worry.

You gave me hope, you gave me strength.

And it feels so good, Better than any wealth.

Somewhere along the path, a part of me messed up.

Brought about bad memories and triggered old cuts.

I know words can't heal our wounds or drown our feelings.

But like any strong bond, words become the seedlings.

I'm sorry for it, I'm sorry that you got scared.

I'm supposed to be your comfort zone, I had declared.

Sometimes we fall, sometimes we do things we don't mean to.

But Delilah, I'll never hurt you, even if the moon turns into two.

You are special, beautiful and amazing.

A rare combination, like a star blazing.

When you are happy, it gives me joys and butterflies.

And I'll do anything to always fix us, no matter how many cries.

You give me the strength to be a better person.

You make me want to open up about each and every aversion.

You are the sun that brightens my day.

I noticed it dimmed down a little, just today.

So, this is my ode, an ode to you.

An ode to apologise, to tell you, my view.

I'm sorry about what I did, and I wish I could take it back.

You won't be alone again; I'll always have your back.

With the apologies done, I see a silver lining.

For me, this brought us closer, it's also a beginning.

A beginning to something stronger, something more beautiful.

You, Delilah, will always be my usual.

# MY WARRIOR PRINCESS

As the sun fades away and darkness settles in.

I begin rewriting this poem, time to begin.

There once was a girl with a heart of gold.

This poem is about her, a story to be told.

We met unexpectedly, a time when I wasn't looking.

Not looking for love or company, just life enduring.

We started talking and connecting, it was magical.

And after a long time, it felt good, it was almost theatrical.

She slowly started to fill my world and my conversations.

Her words were like magic, her eyes created sensations.

Every time I smiled; she was the reason behind it.

And smile I did, a lot after long, I admit.

Soon, my insecurities and fears came back up.

A part of me, afraid, that this will turn to dust.

I opened up to you, told you what I felt.

You made it all go away, almost like it was prepared.

You opened up about your own past and wounds.

That was the day, I fell for you, like a blind fool.

You are gorgeous with a kind and strong soul.

You are everything I ever wanted; you make my life whole.

You are always on my mind; it feels too good to be true.

How can someone so amazing, fall out of the blue.

Her smile brightens my day, her words are music to my soul.

I feel like my heart is a steam engine and she is my coal.

Delilah, you are the key to my missing lock.

I want you to be my last hug, kiss and walk.

A part of my wants to ravish you, a part of me wants to love.

But all of me adores you, you aren't just a crush.

I love how honest you are, how light you make me feel.

Still surprised at how no one ever took you away, what's the deal?

All of this has started to feel better, a lot more real.

My heart is running on overdrive, you are so close to a steal.

I might not know you completely, but I know you enough.

Know where this will go, don't want to rush.

I'm your muse and you make me sing.

You are my warrior princess; I'm waiting with a ring.

# MY FOREVER HABIT

Never had I thought, I would meet her like this.

Somewhere online, I found my lost call.

We instantly clicked, talked a lot that day.

Is this the one? That's the only thought that came to play.

Like her beautiful name, she became my daily habit.

Hearing her endless stories became the favourite thing of my day.

She was so beautiful, especially when she talked about what passionate her.

And I just listened to her, wondering when she could become my forever habit.

Because you see, this is different for me.

It feels like a good friend, a roast, a tease, qualities a lover needs.

I feel I can talk about anything, slowly unfazed my defences.

After all, she's the girl who used her own light to guide me out of darkness.

# BEAUTY IN DELILAH

There once existed a dame, of immense beauty.

She was kind, sweet, precious like a ruby.

My luck charmed; my friend introduced us.

From a game it started, this wonderful rush.

As I got to know her, I started to see things.

I saw how strong she was, how bright she shone, she had wings.

She had scars from past, but she wasn't blinded by the darkness.

She rose back strong from the ashes, without any hardness.

She laughs a lot; her eyes do the talking.

She hides her feelings, so that no one comes knocking.

She lies down at night with hope in her heart.

That someday, a knight will come and take her to the stars.

Stars are where she belongs, like her eyes.

Good news she brings, beauty behind her cries.

She melts the darkness away, like a torch on a cold night.

I only wish she stays happy & I be her supporting knight.

# IS IT ME?

Her smile, one of the most beautiful things in the world.

Her voice, a beautiful thing that needed to be heard.

Endless talks and a heart's connection are what it meant.

Melted away like wax, whisked away without a scent.


I wondered to myself, is it me? Do I care too much?

Am I the reason that turned the smile to frown, am I the cut?

Why so I do this? Why do I hurt the ones I love?

All for naught, I realised, all of the above.


I didn't intent to do it, I never wanted to hurt.

I can't even apologise to her; I don't deserve to be heard.

Where else will I find someone like her, someone who completed me.

Is this the end, is this where I part with, she?


I can't have that; she really means the world to me.

But how do I tell her, do I even deserve the key?

She's too precious for a cobbler like me.

I would leave it all for another day for she.


But is it really me?

I do not want a life without she.

You are precious, remember that always.

And now, I'll leave you alone as I wait in the hallway.


Because I'm sorry, I really am.

I'm sorry because I cared too much, I'm sorry because I'm a sham.

I can't change who I am, you will always be what you are to me.

I'll just wait for you at the horizon because that's where the
sky meets the sea.


You mean the world to me, an earthly promise.

My poetry can't express my fear, remorse or sadness, it's a carcass.

I was wrong, I know, I regret it every day, every hour,
every second.

Don't drift away please, don't feel threatened.


So, with his, I bid you adieu, for a bit.

Come back soon, I miss you, I admit.

Our laughers were contagious and smiles timeless.

I just want that time back again, for me, it was priceless.

# IMAGINE US

I imagine us sitting by the river.

Talking about our dreams, imagine the picture.

I'm holding your hand; I look into your eyes.

All I see is myself and our wedding ties.

I imagine us walking down empty roads.

Little words are spoken, just like those romantic shows.

Comfortable silence and uncontrollable smiles.

That's why I fall for you, you are the candy to my eyes.

I imagine us talking to each other.

Talking about each and everything, no cover.

You blush, you smile, you look like the prettiest girl in the world.

That's when I imagined us together, me and you versus the world.

# BREAKER OF
# THE WALLS

Ever heard of a magical wall, a wall to fend off invaders.

An emotional wall, one that allows you no neighbours.

I had that wall, a huge wall to isolate myself.

Deep in my own misery, I lay waiting, I was reduced to a shell.


Someone came along, someone who showered light.

The darkness withdrew, the skies cleared, it was a beautiful sight.

She walked like an angel, showing me the path.

A path wherein I wasn't alone, a path that had no wrath.

# CAVIAR

A bond is made, more than just the connection.

I never knew I was capable of this, of so much affection.

Little did I know that it will engulf my completely.

However, it was so beautiful, I was hers, incompletely.

I hurt her, I lost her, I loved her, but why.

Why do I do things that made us die.

As I sit and write this, I wonder a lot.

Could things have been different if I knew the plot.

My selfishness caused her to be hurt, my arrogance.

I removed that smile that I loved about her, without any evidence.

She meant the world to me, yet I destroyed her slowly.

It's only now that I realise how incomplete I am, and how she completes me, wholly.

I probably can't have it back; I can't renew our beautiful friendship.

But ishmeet, I have realised and changed, my ways stand mended.

I don't want to hurt you or break you; I simply want that connection.

That connection that first got me you, that perfection.

I sit here writing this poem, half a smile, half a tear.

I can't stop thinking about our beautiful memories, our lovely affair.

And I ask myself, could I have that back, could I speak to her again.

And the answer lies with her as always, for I'm just a leaf and she is my stem.

# AT THE HEART'S JUNCTION

She came like a shooting star, fulfilling my wish.

I had found the one, the chips to my fish.

She complemented me, made me whole.

We were so alike yet different, like a single soul.


Faith turned funny; our hearts beat separately.

Mine continued the same, yours changed parity.

I watched as you walked away, I tried not to cry.

But how can rainbows occur if there aren't any showers in my eyes.


Through my lonely time, I came to say.

Sometimes goodbye is the only way.

I don't want to leave you; I just want to stay.

But my heart beats a different tune, it leads us our separate ways.

# HAPPY BIRTHDAY DELILAH

Some people are born beautiful, pure as white.

They radiate love, they are a divine source of light.

If you meet one, just stay with her for life.

Because this world is a darkness, she can be your eyes.


One such person is you Delilah, you are my light.

Guiding me through darkness, you make me right.

I don't know if I appreciate you enough or tell you how much.

You mean a lot to me, without you, I'll be crushed.


Some people are for forever, some truly connect.

We do Delilah, we truly do have an effect.

You are my anchor and I'm the ship, sailing through eternity.

Let's aim for the horizon, together we go perfectly.


But this isn't about me, it's about you.

It's your birthday, the real beautiful you.

Happy birthday gorgeous, happy birthday to my special one.

Let's hope we last a lifetime, together we aim for the sun.

# EMOTIONAL CATACLYSM

Dark, dark like the silver linings.

Corrupted thy soul, doomed this mortal realm.

See the lightnings, lightnings of this nature.

Hallowed have we become, coarse like the sea.

The loss of my individuality, hammer of society.

Beaten like a rod, heated and moulded my spirit.

Transformed thus, my own self, my cataclysm.

Inferno of the souls, the fire, the cold.

Burned away the human, the inner one.

Left a mortal an, are thy alive?

Made to be a puppet, the strings above.

Opened the pandora, this is the end.

# ODE TO BEAUTY

I saw you walking towards me, like a river you moved.

Calm and swift, your aura had me totally grooved.

I instantly knew she's the one, her perfection mesmerised me.

Oh, how I wish to hold her, how I wish to be her sea.

Like the lone lighthouse on a dark sea.

You brought me light and home, you are the key.

The locks and shackles that trap my soul and spirit.

You freed me up, I had never felt something so illicit.

Whenever we talk Delilah, my heart skips a few beats.

I lose track of time; your eyes are like a drug to me.

If I could only, have you, just you for a single day.

It'd be worth a thousand years of pain, a price I'm willing to pay.

You complete me, you make me happy.

I hope I can do the same, nothing too fancy.

The heart is a spirit and our soul a road.

I have found my destination; will you climb aboard?

I feel so deeply for you, this intensity unknown.

I only wish you to know, you will never be alone.

SHEIBBAN SHEIKH PERVEZ

I'll always be here, day, night like a banshee.

Date me already, so that I can finally bend on my knee.

# MENTAL SCHISM

The mind, the fuel of the fire within.

Burns like a crippling skin of the once been.

Connections of the heart, the soul of the temple.

Pieces have been scattered, the schism of the mental.


The path beyond lies confused and profound.

Irony exists, like the nightingale without sound.

Beautiful the confusion is this chaos.

It emits the schism of our reality, our pathos.


Can't we be connected, connected with the soul.

Is the dissonance so strong, it shatters us whole?

This feeling, this emotion, this mental schism.

It's the culmination, the cold birth of the organism.

# BEATING OF MY HEART

Have you ever looked at something, something so divine?

It caused your heart to skip a beat, it made your soul alive.

Words get trapped, your eyes flushed, throat parched.

Blood pumps up, her eyes and your heart.

Her name is Delilah, golden like the sun.

Perfect in her own way, perfect to be the one.

I want to hold her, kiss her, tell her.

That no matter what happens, I'll be here for her.

She's the girl you find once in a lifetime.

I'm so lucky to realise this, I don't want to waste any time.

Having her would make me complete, like parts to a puzzle.

After all, all couples are made in heaven, the world is our bubble.

So, I have found her, my better half, the shining knight.

I'm standing here, holding a candle, hoping she sees the light.

Days turn into months, months into years, years into a lifetime.

But I'll always adore her, she's my heart's guideline.

Let's try our luck, let's fall together.

One last time, one last try, altogether.

What is life if not a madness, hold my hand as we dive.

I promise I'll love you, from this day until we die.

# THE GOLDEN GIRL

Some people live, some people thrive.

Some people pass, some they glide.

Some are courageous, they are the victory.

That's the golden girl, she's my heart's artery.


Some people are so beautiful, they shine the stars away.

They make their own ambience; they command their own day.

That's Delilah for you, the one with the golden heart.

Her smile can defeat a thousand evils and that's just the start.


Anyone would fall her, anyone with a pair of eyes.

She's mesmerising in her own way; she gives your heart a little rise.

Time flies by as you sit and talk to her for days and nights.

It's only then you realise, your life is a darkness and she's the light.


The way she talks, the way she is, it's like the morning dew.

Subtle and calming, she brings out the real you.

She's so caring, so kind, her eyes deep like the ocean.

It brings out the best in you, the purest emotion.


But this story isn't about me, it's about the birthday girl.

I just couldn't help it, I had to describe my pearl.

Happy birthday Delilah, Here's to a new start.

Happy birthday to the one and only, the girl with the golden heart.

# SNOW HEART

Pink lips, sweet smile, long hair.
Waves the girl while not giving a care.
Magnificent she is words can't describe her.
Her name is Delilah, like the pure winter wind.

She walks shielded, there's hardly any room.
No room to hurt or no room to loom?
How beautiful it is, indeed.
When all I want is her company in need.

She smiles like the brightest stars.
Her scars unshown, behind locked bars.
She laughs like there's no end, no start.
A heart pure as white, a snow heart.

# SIX DEGREES OF LOVE

Seasons change, the temperature slowly falls.

Mornings are longer, my heart transcends the walls.

You are beautiful, undeniably so.

I have undeniably fallen for you, just so you know.

Every day I wake up to your smiling face.

Your lovely hair, your gorgeous eyes.

Your radiant personality, the one that makes me weak.

Weak at the heart, weak like a freak.

I can't stop thinking about you, I really can't.

I imagine us together, from now till in hand.

You are my past, my present, my future.

So how about dating me? Making me cuter?

# SUNNY DAYS

Ever since you were a child, you had a dream.

A dream of a future, dream to be seen.

I had mine; I spent my whole life searching.

I finally found you, for whom my heart is burning.

I feel for you Delilah, I really do.

Give me a chance, together we two.

We will conquer the world, rule like kings.

The sky is the limit, we have no wings.

I don't deserve you; you are too good to be true.

You are perfect Delilah, the one who makes me you.

I'm serious about this, always have and will be.

I have found my calling, here's my plea.

I like you; I truly do.

Not just your perfections but the real you.

I'm ready to wait, to get hurt, to be disappointed.

Because that will make me the luckiest man, together and always.

# LOBSTER

My whole life had been a long search.

A search for a girl, one who won't hurt.

This girl of my dreams, beautiful and amazing.

She's the kind you want to wake up next to, gazing.

I'm not the person who can leave you or hurt you.

I love you now, I'll always love you.

I know you are a bit broken; I know it all.

But Delilah trust me, I'll be there for the fall.

I want to fix you; I want to get you back to life.

I can honestly say that I'll make you, my wife.

You are the girl of my dreams, always have and always will be.

And I have always been that for you, just you and me.

Everyone has that one person who is their guardian.

You make me so radioactive, like thorium.

Who says that dreams can't come true, who says you have to be practical?

I'm telling you Delilah; I have always been this radical.

We spend our entire lives searching for the one.

I have found mine; I have won.

You are the dove that has unlocked my locker.

After all Delilah, you are my lobster.

# ETERNAL HORIZON

Like the brightest stars in the sky.

Your eyes are what makes me so high.

Candle, candle, you are the light to my darkness.

You keep me whole, just like the strongest harness.

The gorgeous princess or the ravishing queen.

You are the only lady of my dreams.

Your voice gives me power, it gives me hope.

You are like my life's piano's missing note.

If my heart was a kingdom, you would be the queen and its ruler.

Even your thought makes me smile over and over.

I wish we were like two rocks sitting at the beach.

Looking at passing sunsets and aiming for the horizon to reach.

# RAINS OF AMOUR

Friends come, some stay, some go.

You have always been there for me, just so you know.

Trust is hard to build, friendship harder to maintain.

But now that I have you, there is not left to obtain.


Everyone has a dark knight, a hidden guardian.

If it was a competition, you would be my champion.

You have always been there and supported from the shadows.

You mean so much to me, I'd always protect you, even from a
million arrows.


Whenever my life became a desert, you were the rain.

Always helping me and eradicating my pain.

I might have a million girlfriends or just one with whom I'll be.

But you always be in my heart, you mean the world to me.

# CARNIVAL OF DESIRES

Little boy, big boy, old man, young man.

We all wonder where our one woman is.

People send their life searching for their desires.

They all say they truly love them, a bunch of liars.


If you truly love something, they would be yours.

What a girl truly wants is your heart, not your lures.

Every girl wants a guy who loves her to bits.

But little does she realise; he had always been it.


Why can't we look past ourselves, our own limits?

Let's create a bond that links our very spirits.

The world thinks the ideal romance is Romeo and Juliet.

How about we show them it's Delilah and Sheibban, let's make this duet.

# DELILAH AND ME

Like the brightest stars in the sky.

Your eyes are what makes me so high.

Candle, candle, you are the light to my darkness.

You keep me whole, just like the strongest harness.

The gorgeous princess or the ravishing queen.

You are the only lady of my dreams.

Your voice gives me power, it gives me hope.

You are like my life's piano's missing note.

You are my Delilah, I'm your peach.

Even your thought makes me smile over and over.

I wish we were like two rocks sitting at the beach.

Looking at passing sunsets and aiming for the horizon to reach.

# MEETING DELILAH

I saw you the first day of my college.

It seemed like I had found a long-lost locket.

You were extremely pretty, stunningly beautiful.

You just seemed so perfect or was I delusional.

We used to talk, a little here, a little there.

I wish we talked more, there was a flare.

Finally, we became good friends, I had you close now.

I will always care and protect you, that's my vow.

I find you very sweet, very desirable.

You are totally out of my league, it's not even viable.

You are like the beautiful diamond found at last.

You can shine just like a star, shining brightness, removing overcast.

So, tell me what you want to hear.

I have no more secrets, nothing left to endear.

You are amazing, beautiful and perfect.

You command every guy's love and his respect.

# MY EVERYTHING

Just like a guitar to a musician.

You are the heart to my position.

I can imagine being with you forever.

But even then, we won't have much time, am not I clever?


Recently we have fought, we have changed, we have survived.

This love that we share has been broken and revived.

You are like a proton and I'm an electron, together we make
an atom.

I guess opposites really do attract, can't you imagine.


Friends for life, lovers for beyond.

That's my dream with you babe, why don't you respond.

I never want to force you for anything, except 50 shades.

But even then, you will be my everything, from diamonds to
spades.


How about some sugar then, how about a date?

Just me and you, together are our fate.

You can cuddle with me; you can act all crazy.

Cause I'll always be there for you Delilah, you are my daisy.

# MY HEART'S NIGHTINGALE

There was a girl, a girl of gold.

She had the most beautiful eyes; I had been told.

I got to know her through a friend, amazing she was.

I fell in love at first sight, without a cause.


Then started our journey, as friends and lovers.

I still want to know her more; she has many wonders.

Her name is Delilah, it's amazing as her.

I'm sometimes surprised that such a thing can actually occur.


We have had a long history, a strong chemistry.

But you are like my love potion, my remedy.

I'm so crazy about you, you my everything.

You are my winter queen, I'm your summer king.


The thing I love the most is your cute little smile.

I have been thinking something, I have been thinking awhile.

Let's just end this game of cat and mouse.

Get dressed up and ready, make our vows?

I know you might want to wait; I know you aren't ready.
But Delilah if there is ever a time, now be my teddy.
This new year is the time that I seek and want.
I'm looking forward to forever strengthening our bond.

I want to date you, Delilah; I want to be yours.
Nothing else makes sense to me, I'm ready to endure.
I'll love you till the end of time, before and after.
All I am now waiting for is your final answer.

I'm not a perfect person, I'm not what you deserve.
But I promise I'll change; I promise I'll inverse.
If a poem could be a will, this is my love.
So, tell me now Delilah, will you be my dove.

# BOX OF LOVE



Everyone has their own little box of love.

Some call it the heart; some call it their rush.

It has all our secrets, our desires, our emotions.

It shapes our being, defining our very own notions.


But as with a box, it must have a key.

It's more like a cryptex, the code word being we.

You and I are so beautiful, we define our very own box.

This chemistry that we have, it's like the shackles to our locks.


I wouldn't mind being bonded to one person forever.

But some things Delilah, are meant to be together.

Just like you and me cutie, we are meant to be.

So, let's just be together my love, you complete me.

# TWO STARS

A jet-black night, a million lights.

I look up to the sky, I see heavenly sprites.

Every star stands for a person, ever twinkle a life.

All of them stay together, until the sunrise.

No star is alone, no person is forlorn.

Even if all the stars vanish, one special one will be born.

Some relations are forever, some are like our deepest scars.

They will always endure; they are like our twinkling stars.

You are special to me, always have and always will be.

Even if the earth shifts, I'll be there, you and me.

You will never be alone, you have shaggy.

So don't you ever be sad again, I'll make you happy.

# MY PRINCESS



Twinkle twinkle little stars.

You are the cure to all my scars.

My heart, my mind, my body, my soul.

You are the only person that makes me whole.

The sea has fishes, the sky has stars.

Sometimes I wonder if you are from mars.

How can someone be so perfect, so pure?

Just one look at you is all my cure.

I know I messed up; I know I suck.

But Delilah you are so beautiful, I really need a lot of luck

You are the best thing to ever happen to me.

And I swear to you, one day I'll bend for you on my knee.

# THE GIRL WITH THE GOLDEN HEART

Everyone is a different person, everyone a different face.

Everyone trying to survive, everyone finding their own space.

Between all that falseness, all that boulevard.

Lies our cherry, the girl with the golden heart.

You have a pleasant and a smile too cute.

If the world was a tree, you would be its sweetest fruit.

I wish we were friends ever since we started school.

Because not only are you so fun to talk to, you are so cool.

A girl's beauty lies in her eyes and her heart.

You have both, like the perfect star.

We might drift apart someday or get close even more.

But I would always remember you, the one with innocence at her core.

# STRAWBERRY SUNSHINE

If strawberries were a colour, id paint my whole world with it.

It would look so beautiful just like when you smile with your cute little lips.

Everyone was born a couple; we look for our heart's line.

But now that I have met you, I know, you are my strawberry sunshine.


You, you are so beautiful.

I've fallen in love with you, totally irrevocable.

If you could be my sun, you would shine everything so bright.

But no matter what happens, you would always be the star of my night.


The hardest things to obtain are always the most valuable.

You are that to me, you make me totally irrational.

This feeling you ooze, it feels so divine.

You my love, are my strawberry sunshine.

# SMILING FLAME

There was once a fire, it was a close friend.

She was sweet and innocent, a perfect blend.

One day I hurt her, wasn't my intention.

I was sorry and I apologised but it was too late for my intervention.


Upset she was, lost her smile she did.

I didn't feel good, I only meant to kid.

That sweet smiling light vanished suddenly.

If only I could turn back time and get her company.


Like the sun, she emitted light.

Shining high, it was so bright.

I wondered what I should do to make it up to her.

This is just a sorry message saying I'm so immature.

# THE MASTERPIECE

When God was at work.

He created a masterpiece.

Something that made my heart berserk.

You were my missing piece.

When I talk to you.

I can't help but smile.

We are perfect, we two.

You make my senses mistime.

If I could have a penny each time, I said your name.

I would be the richest man alive.

Not because I'll have all the money and fame.

But because I'll have you, my biggest prize.

The way you speak, the way you talk.

You make my heart skip a beat.

My thought process becomes so analogue.

It's as if, you make me complete.

But what I really love about you.

Isn't your beauty or your looks.

SHEIBBAN SHEIKH PERVEZ

It's your simplicity that makes our glue.
It's your heart that makes me hooked.

# HARMONY

If my heart was a lock, you would be the key.

Nothing else matters except together we be.

Like the flowers of the first spring, beautiful you are.

You don't know how much I love you; you are my shooting star.


We have stopped talking a bit, due to certain reasons

Let's change that Delilah, become each other's needles.

I want to be addicted to you, not alcohol or drugs.

Because you are so amazing, you just make my heart go blush.


I think we are perfect, like fraise and noel.

Let's stick together, become each other's gel.

Just remember there is always someone here waiting for you.

So, no matter how worse things are, I'll always be the cherry pour vous.

# NOTHING ELSE MATTERS

When you are with me.
It's something to be seen.
Everything is so magical.
Nothing else is meant to be.

I remember the sky.
I remember the stars.
I look upon them.
You are what is all I see.

If love was a blessing.
You would be my angel.
Together we sing.
The song of our mingle.

When I look upon you.
It's as if time stops.
Nothing else matters.
You are my heart's clock.

# MY NORTHERN LIGHT



When I gaze upon the skies.
The stars, they seem so high.
As I look up on the mighty sight.
I realise Delilah, you are my northern light.

Brighter than the skies.
Brighter than any smile.
Everything about you.
Radiates of life.

We have been friends since long.
Everything so perfect, feels like a song.
I am no pop band Delilah but.
I just want to be with you until my eyes shut.

# TOGETHER

One day, I saw someone.

Someone so beautiful, it felt like she is the one.

Didn't have thoughts to think or words to speak.

Little did I know that you would be everything that I seek.

I asked, what makes you so beautiful?

Your eyes, they captured my entire soul.

But what gave me away wasn't anything I had seen before.

It was your smile, my love, which I wanted more and more.

Together we are but still far apart.

You know I love you, don't tempt my heart.

Just say yes once, once more.

And I will show you how deep my world goes.

# BROKEN



Like the shorts of a diamond.

My heart, it was a Big Island.

An island full of love, surrounded by despair.

Only my friends could come because they care.

I thought friendship was a gift.

A blitz, a beautiful kiss.

Never have I felt so wrong, so broken.

Everything felt like it was stolen.

Some friends, I thought were eternal.

Some still are, some just a hurdle.

Friendships can either make you or break you.

For me, it was just like the morning dew.

# PERFECTION

If I could define you in one word.
The word would be perfect.
Just like an exotic rare bird.
You, my love, are priceless.

I don't know if you love me or not.
I don't know if you care about me or not.
I don't know if we will be together or never.
But what I know is that I will love you till forever.

You have my heart, your time and space.
If love was a vessel, you would be my vase.
The only other woman I would say I love you to.
Wouldn't be anyone but the daughter of me and you.

# TIME

My time with you feels like a song.

Each moment so pure, so long.

I would rather be with you than a thousand fairies.

That's because I love you, my dear cherry.


I wish we age together, like an exotic wine.

Everything becomes more beautiful; it is so divine.

If I could love you, even until forever.

It still won't be enough because you are my greatest treasure.


I wish upon the skies; you be with me.

Together on a road, towards our destiny.

Crossing rivers and deserts, till we are free.

Only then can we love, until eternity.

# COME AND GOES

Somethings come and go.

Illness, it totally blows.

Just like the seasons and the wind.

These things always leave you in a bind.

Love and care can achieve miracles.

Nothing can ever seem so horrible.

You are ill now but get well soon.

It will come and go, just like the typhoons.

# KINSHIP

The ghastly meadows of the widow's heart.
The silent drums of a child cry.
The empty whistle of a lover's rose.
The dying hope of a soldier's plight.

Vast, hollow bodies scavenging the earth.
Searching for their love, searching for a soul.
Like a broken compass, we continue to move.
Hoping for the harbour, expecting the moon.

As the journey continues, the feelings deepen.
Our heart grow stronger, but the mind weakens.

# IT WILL RAIN AGAIN

It will rain again.
The farmer said after the draught.
Ploughed and cried, with all his heart.
He knew this is in life, it's just a part.

Like the candle dries away the darkness.
Sometimes it's the little things that seem harmless.
But just as a candle can become a flame.
The ones who hurt us are whose hearts we reign.

Gifted other people who experience love.
It completes their life, just like an artist and his brush.
You, you are beautiful, smart and caring.
But it's the heart that makes you and it can't be tearing.

Like an albatross guiding sailors to their paths.
You are the beacon of light in my dark star.
The beacon is shrivelling, the flame going weak.
Things are shaken, she couldn't find what she seeks.

Just like how you drive away the darkness.
It's now my time to be the charm.

Even if hell freezes over, I will keep you warm.

I'll be the brightest star to guide you come back to she.

And if the flames end up burning me, that will be my destiny.

# FOR WHAT IS?

The language of love, is it not to expect?

Is it not to dream about us? Is it not to think?

About a future with you? Is it not to embrace you?

In my arms until you cry your heart out?

For me love is to love, it is to love blindly and deeply.

Like the books of Hemingway or Shakespeare.

It is to accept your reality and how enchanted we are.

But, to get that we must let go of that which makes us, us.

We need to stop thinking, stop thinking about love.

Feel it instead, feel the energy enveloped you.

Feel it in the air and do not overthink, for it is only then.

Are we our real selves, capable of real love?

On a dark summer night, our thoughts often very.

The past is sought, our hearts uneasy, thirsty we are.

For the same love and affection that once bonded us.

Now becomes the shackle to her hearts, restricting us.

Heal we shall, in our own time, space and thought shine.

Endless scenarios we plan from each interaction, blinded.

Compared to our own true self, we become only a shadow.

Remains of our originality, let's be whole again.

# YOU AND ME

The day I saw you.
My heart skipped a beat.
You were standing there, looking at books.
My heart told me it's destiny.

We started talking all day long.
Each moment, so pure.
We became friends and got closer
Much more, soon to be.

I fell in love, uncontrollable and unconditional.
I just knew, it was meant to be.
Ask you out, I did, confessing my love.
You remained unsure, unseen?
Left alone I was.

We tried to work it out, little progress made.
Fought like the gods, hurt we both were.
We distanced away, more and more.
But our hearts still longed each other.

Some years past, we started talking again.

Rediscovering each other, a beautiful thing.

What soon appeared was in friendship or love.

But it was more beautiful than anything I had ever seen.

We started falling for each other.

This time, determined to be.

And now again, we stand at the crossroads.

Will you go out with me?

Love you I have, love you I will.

Nothing has ever made more sense to me.

I know that you don't trust me, because of a past.

But I promise you, you will always be with me.

My heart belongs to you, always has been.

I just want you to be happy.

Nothing else fazes me.

You are like an Angel, in my darkness.

Shining light just like the sun at its brightest.

Everything about you pleases me.

Your beauty, your intelligence is so unseen.

I can't help but fall in love.

I just hope, you be with me.

So once again, I stand before you.

On my knees, I am.

Humbly asking you to be.

Once again, the jewel for me.

If love is a river, you are my ocean.
Swimming in it till eternity.
Everything seems a dream, nothing feels finite
This moment, we are infinite.

# ELEMENTS



Eyes, bright as the sky.

Lips, red as the evening sun.

Hair, flowing like the river.

Smile, glowing as the stars.

Cheeks, like the autumn.

Nose, perfect as the earth.

Personality, stern like the wind.

Attitude, fiery as fire.

Style, growing like nature.

You, unlike any other.

# THE LAST GAME

The seasons change, leaves change colour.

Time loses its essence, it's life in technicolour.

People are like nature, they come, and they go.

Some last forever, they are the ones who grow.


I walked a lonely road, a road without signs.

I walked every day, every-hour, I followed the lines.

I was blinded you see, blinded by my own nature.

When your shields are so up, it's time for the sabre.


You woke me up, you guided me through the road.

I know you since a long time, how come I never noticed?

The most beautiful things are sometimes right in front of you.

In my case, it's been you, it's always been you.


I close my eyes; I think about my life.

All I can see is a picture with you in my eyes.

Is this special? Am I in love?

A thousand questions arise, where does that leave us?


I have been hurt a lot before, I'm full of wounds.

These wounds, they bleed, they are my heart's tunes.

I have managed to cover them up, cover them all.

But for you, I'm ready to once again fall.

Who knows where we are today, yesterday or tomorrow?

The destination is uncertain, the path furrow.

All we have is our body and soul.

Along with that special one, the one who makes me whole.

For me, it's you, you are my light.

I know all this is very emotional, I'm sorry for the write.

I feel for you lady, truly, madly, deeply.

I just want to offer you the world maybe, I'm yours completely.

I understand that we aren't the closest of people, the closest of friends.

So how can we fall for each other, who sets the trends?

I don't have the answers, only questions instead.

But I know for certain, you are the equity to my debt.

Roses and lilies, the skies and diamonds.

All things have a meaning, until the horizon.

Even the nature acknowledges this, it gives meaning to a season.

Just like you give to me, you are my reason.

You make me want to be a better person, a better human being.

You bring out the passion in me, the passion to really start
freeing.

Freeing from this facedness, this abnormality.

Wake up and see you next to me, that's my reality.

I have never written such a thing before, never have and
never will.

You are really special to me; you are now and till death until.

I'm just a guy on his knees telling you, his feelings.

All I expect is a hearing, all I want is our meaning.


Think about this for a second, think about the future.

A guy who thinks the world of you, a guy who could be the suitor.

I don't know if you believe in love, I don't know if you are
ready today.

But for someone like you, I'll wait a thousand days.


You are the girl I want to woo; you are the one I want.

Movies, pasta and rum, which could be our own little bond.

You make me happy; you make me want to live.

I haven't felt this way in a while, I really feel the drift.


We have a connection, I believe, we have a natural spark.

You are intelligent, smart and beautiful, I'm the other end of
the park.

I probably don't deserve an amazing person like you but
let me try my luck.

After all, life is all about chances, I want you to be my last hug.


I have played games all my life, chasing and replacing.

I'm tired of that, I'm tired of this racing.

I want to end that now, settle for the perfect dame.

I have finally found her; this is my last game.

# ABOUT THE AUTHOR

I am a poet with a passion for romantic works. My personal favourite poem is the "Road Not Taken" by Robert Frost. It is one of the poems that has tremendously helped me over the years during difficult situations by showing me a way out.

The poems contained in this book were written over several years ever since I can remember writing. Some were written during my school days while majority were written while I was in college.

I currently live in New Delhi. I have an undergraduate degree in engineering and a master's in business management. Other than writing, I also enjoy listening to non-fiction audiobooks.

I enjoy playing music and have been learning the piano and the violin. Swimming and Chess are two of my favourite sports. I love animals, currently have two lovely indies who are always excited to meet new people!

I like long walks and mountain treks. There is just something innately beautiful about exploring mountain trails across several days and being in sync with nature. I happen to be a huge anime fan (borderline nerd) with a particular passion for Shonen manga.

# Space For You To Write Your Own Poetry